CLASS ASSEMBLIES 1

Ready-to-use assemblies for whole-class performances

D1797688

Veronica Clark
Kaye Umansky
Pippa Goodhart
Jenny McLachlan

Contents

Introduction

Class Assemblies 1 contains everything you need to put on a successful class performance; perfect for whole-class assemblies or an end of term production for a wider audience.

The book contains:
- scripts/stories
- curriculum-based activities
- links to SEAL and literacy units
- performance tips
- melody lines for the songs

The CD contains:
- sung performances and backing tracks to sing along with
- incidental music to use in your performance (including entry and exit music for each assembly)

Whatever your resources, and whether you are aiming for something large scale, or simple and basic, this book will help you to stage a successful performance. The title page of each story provides a quick overview of the cast, story, theme and songs, and the performance notes and stage plans supply further ideas for rehearsing and staging the assembly stories.

The assemblies aim to be as flexible as possible. Although the four plays are designed for a specific age group, they can be adapted for use with other age groups.

You could present the plays as stories for use in the classroom to prompt discussion. The *Literacy Links* boxes show where you could incorporate the stories into literacy work. Each play is based around a simple moral or message, which is explored in the PSHE notes in the *Curriculum Links* section and outlined on the title page.

Preparing for the assembly

Familiarise the children with the play by reading it through a couple of times, like a story, and then discuss it with the class (see PSHE notes and *SEAL Links*). Work through some of the activities in the *Curriculum Links*. Involve the children in collecting and making props and costumes.

Take the opportunity to introduce children to new vocabulary, for example, **cast**, **props**, **scenery**, **scripts**.

Casting

Numbers for various parts are approximate, and are based on an average class size of 30. Adapt to suit your class. Some of the parts involve the children remembering lines. Make sure that the children are familiar with the cues to their lines in the narration, and encourage them to project their voices and avoid turning away from the audience when they are speaking or singing. Discuss the characters the children are playing and help them to give a convincing performance. If children have trouble remembering their lines, consider attaching their text to a prop, or incorporate some of the lines into the narration.

Staging and performance tips

Adapt these to suit your needs. You can ignore, embellish, adapt or simplify them.

Stage directions such as **stage back left** or **stage front right** are interpreted by imagining you are standing on the stage facing the audience (see also *Stage Plans*).

The stage plans show starting positions, where to put props and scenery, and the movement around the stage area.

Venue and acting space

The notes assume the plays are being performed in a large room, such as a hall. Adapt to your circumstances.

The word **stage** refers to the main performance area. This can either be a designated area of floor space or a raised stage. Teachers using a raised stage will need between one and three sets of steps for movement on and off the stage.

References to **off stage** and **below the stage** describe space outside the main performance area. Where a raised stage is being used, they refer to activity at floor level.

The stage plans

The stage plans at the back of the book are drawn on squared backgrounds. Each square represents one square metre. Adapt the plans to suit your needs.

It may sometimes be helpful to use tape or chalk to show children where to stand and the routes they take.

Costumes

Costume suggestions are given in the performance notes. For a smaller-scale production, simplify the costumes, or consider using only one element, eg, headdresses. Adding noses, whiskers, spots, etc, using face paints, can add an exciting dimension to performances.

Storytellers (narrators)

An adult will need to perform the narration. Spoken lines written for individual children can be incorporated into the storyteller's part if necessary.

Songs and chants

The songs in this pack are catchy and easy to learn: some consist of new words to well-known tunes, and some are simple original songs.

Sound effects

A group of children could be chosen to make any necessary sound effects. If you do so, reduce the number of cast members without speaking parts.

Magic in the Classroom
by Veronica Clark

Cast
Storyteller (adult)
Miss Parr, the class teacher
Geraldine and Fred
Melanie
Amie West and Jack
Miss Parr's class (about 24)
Classroom assistant/helper (optional)

The children in the cast play themselves. The words spoken by Miss Parr can either be read by the narrator, or by an adult taking the part of the teacher. Five children have special parts to play, but no individual lines to speak.

Assembly theme

The focus of *Magic in the Classroom* is on developing good listening skills, and encouraging children to do as they are asked. The negative aspects of not listening are demonstrated, as are the positive effects of co-operative behaviour.

Story

Magic in the Classroom describes a day in the life of a class and their teacher, Miss Parr. In the first part of the story, the school day is spoilt for everyone because four children don't listen to their teacher.

Instead of clearing up their toys, Geraldine and Fred throw their Lego™ bricks around. Then, dreamy Melanie is so absorbed in her book that she stays behind in the classroom when everyone else goes out for a fire drill. Finally, Amie disrupts story time by fooling around at the back of the class.

Miss Parr's wish that the day could start again comes true. We are magicked back to 10.30 in the morning and, second time round, the day goes like clockwork, because the children listen and do as they are asked straight away.

Setting

The story is set in the classroom. In Scene 2, the children leave the stage for the fire drill. In the re-run of the school day, this is omitted.

Songs and chants

There are three songs, two of which are based on traditional tunes. *What a pity* is repeated several times. Everyone can speak the chants (which are in bold, large-case letters). However, one child with a loud voice could speak the three opening and closing couplets.

Script: Magic in the Classroom

Scene 1: A busy classroom   Time: 10.00am

**THIS PLAY IS ALL ABOUT A RULE
WELL-KNOWN TO EVERYONE IN SCHOOL.**

**ALWAYS LISTEN WHEN IN CLASS,
AND TRY TO DO AS YOU ARE ASKED.**

**LET'S MEET THE ACTORS. COME INSIDE –
THE CLASSROOM DOOR IS OPEN WIDE.**

(ACTION – A CLOCK IN THE CLASSROOM SHOWS 10.00.)

CD 2/11

SONG: A BUSY CLASSROOM (*The Farmer's in his den*)

We're playing in the sand,
We're playing in the sand.
We're having fun today,
We're playing in the sand.

We're looking at some books ...

We're playing with the cars ...

We're playing with the bricks ...

We're threading wooden beads ...

We're serving in the shop ...

We're mixing up the paint ...

▶

⏸ Forward to
next track

(ACTION – THE CLOCK HANDS ARE MOVED TO 10.30.)

STORYTELLER
The clock was showing half past ten.
Miss Parr clapped ... then clapped again.

TEACHER
Listen please. It's time to stop.
Sweep up the sand and close the shop.

Pick up your toys and clear away.
There's just five minutes left 'til play.

STORYTELLER
The children stopped, and, keen to please,
Buzzed around like busy bees.

(ACTION – THE CHILDREN, WITH THE EXCEPTION OF GERALDINE AND
FRED, TIDY AWAY THEIR PLAY EQUIPMENT IN THEIR GROUPS.)

The sand was swept, the shop was shut,
No more paint or dressing up.

Shelves were stacked with toys and books,
Painting aprons went on hooks.

Two children, Geraldine and Fred,
Had not done what Miss Parr said.

(SOUND EFFECT – CYMBAL ROLL.)

UH-OH, TROUBLE! SOMETHING'S WRONG.
LET'S FIND OUT WHAT'S GOING ON.

Thinking they were out of sight,
They'd started up a Lego™ fight.

Bricks flew here, bricks flew there.
Miss Parr fixed them with a stare.

Forward to
next track

SONG: WHAT A PITY (*Clementine*)

What a pity, what a pity,
It's no fun at school today.
One or two won't stop to listen
To what the teacher has to say.

(ACTION – DURING THE SONG, GERALDINE AND FRED CLEAR AWAY
THE LEGO™.)

At last the two cleared up their toys,
Then joined the other girls and boys.

TEACHER
I'm really very sad to say,
You've missed the whole of morning play.

(ACTION – EVERYONE GROANS AND LOOKS DEJECTED.)

MUSIC: **SAD PLAYTIME MUSIC** (*Girls and boys go out to play*)

(ACTION – DURING THE SAD PLAYTIME MUSIC, THE CHILDREN SLOWLY
STAND UP AND GATHER IN FRONT OF THEIR TEACHER, SITTING WITH
THEIR BACKS TO THE AUDIENCE.)

Scene 2: Fire drill   Time: 11.00am

(ACTION – THE CLOCK NOW SHOWS 11.00.)

Playtime over, work begun.
The theme was Safety in the Sun.

But then the bell rang, loud and shrill.
Everyone went very still.

(SOUND EFFECT – THE FIRE BELL RINGS OFFSTAGE.)

TEACHER
Stand up children. That's the sign
To leave the building. Make a line.

(ACTION – ALL CHILDREN EXCEPT MELANIE STAND UP AND LEAD OFF IN A LINE.)

STORYTELLER
Outside Miss Parr looked all around –
Good. Her class was safe and sound.

She ticked their names off on a list
To make sure nobody was missed.

She frowned, then checked the list again.
There was no tick by just one name.

(SOUND EFFECT – CYMBAL ROLL.)

Script – MAGIC IN THE CLASSROOM

UH-OH, TROUBLE! SOMETHING'S WRONG. LET'S FIND OUT WHAT'S GOING ON.

Mel was missing. Miss Parr sighed.
She left the class and went inside.

(ACTION – MISS PARR RETURNS TO THE CLASSROOM TO LOOK FOR MELANIE.)

Back in class, she looked around;
It seemed deserted – not a sound.

She peeped behind the library chair,
And can you guess whom she found there?

On a cushion, tightly curled,
Was Melanie, lost to the world.

Her head was full of kings and queens,
Monsters, teddies, magic scenes.

REPEAT SONG: WHAT A PITY

What a pity, what a pity ...

(ACTION – DURING THE SONG, MELANIE LEAVES THE BOOK CORNER AND JOINS THE OTHER CHILDREN. AT THE END OF THE SONG, THE CHILDREN WALK BACK ON STAGE AND SIT FACING THE TEACHER AS BEFORE. THEY TALK QUIETLY AMONGST THEMSELVES. AMIE AND JACK SIT AT THE BACK, IN THE MIDDLE.)

Scene 3: Story time   Time: 2.30pm

(ACTION – THE CLOCK NOW SHOWS 2.30.)

At half past two, the children sat
In one big group upon the mat.

TEACHER
First a story, then a song.
Settle down, we haven't long.

(ACTION – THE CHILDREN STOP TALKING AND LOOK AT MISS PARR.)

STORYTELLER

When all was quiet, Miss Parr told
A tale about a princess bold,

Who climbed a tower, kissed a toad,
And met a dragon on the road.

A noise disturbed her. At the back,
Amie West was shoving Jack.

Miss Parr sighed and looked around.
She heard a little sniggering sound.

(SOUND EFFECT – CYMBAL ROLL.)

UH-OH, TROUBLE! SOMETHING'S WRONG.
LET'S FIND OUT WHAT'S GOING ON.

TEACHER

Who's being silly? Amie West,
You're spoiling it for all the rest.

REPEAT SONG: WHAT A PITY

What a pity, what a pity ...

Forward to
next track

(THE CLOCK SHOWS 3.00.)

STORYTELLER

Miss Parr was sad when home time came.

TEACHER

It really, really is a shame,

I've had to grumble and complain.
I wish that we could start again!

Scene 4: Magic in the classroom

STORYTELLER
The room went quiet – all was still.
Time went backwards, past the drill,

Past play and milk to half past ten,
And then the day began again.

(ACTION – THE MAGIC MUSIC GROUP PLAYS. DURING THE MAGIC
MUSIC, THE CLOCK HANDS ARE MOVED BACKWARDS UNTIL THEY
SHOW 10.30, AND THE CHILDREN MOVE SLOWLY TO THEIR STARTING
POSITIONS AND START PLAYING AGAIN.)

Scene 1 reprise: A busy classroom   Time: 10.30am

TEACHER
Listen please. It's time to stop.
Sweep up the sand and close the shop.

Pick up your toys and clear away.
There's just five minutes left 'til play.

STORYTELLER
The children stopped, and, keen to please,
Buzzed around like busy bees.

The sand was swept, the shop was shut,
No more paint or dressing up.

Shelves were stacked with toys and books,
Painting aprons went on hooks.

Fred and Gerry, on the floor,
Put their Lego™ in the drawer.

Everyone did as they were asked.
Miss Parr said, `WHAT A LOVELY CLASS!´

SONG: HAPPY DAYS (*Original*)

Forward to next track

If we all do as we're asked,
And do it straight away,
We don't waste time,
We learn a lot,
And have a happy day.
We don't waste time,
We learn a lot,
And have a happy day.

Scene 2 reprise: Fire drill   Time: 11.00am

(ACTION – THE CLOCK SHOWS 11.00.)

Playtime over, work begun.
The theme was Safety in the Sun.

But then the bell rang, loud and shrill.
Everyone went very still.

Melanie was first in line.
She didn't waste a bit of time.

Outside Miss Parr looked all around –
Good. Her class was safe and sound.

Everyone did as they were asked.
Miss Parr said, `**WHAT A LOVELY CLASS!**´

Forward to next track

REPEAT SONG: HAPPY DAYS

If we all do as we're asked ...

Scene 3 reprise: Story time   Time: 2.30pm

(ACTION – THE CLOCK SHOWS 2.30.)

At half past two, the children sat
In one big group upon the mat.

TEACHER
First a story, then a song.
Settle down, we haven't long.

STORYTELLER
When all was quiet, Miss Parr told
A tale about a princess bold.

Who climbed a tower, kissed a toad,
And met a dragon on the road.

They fought. The princess smote him dead,
Then went to find a prince to wed.

Amie listened very well,
They had two songs before the bell.

Everyone did as they were asked.
Miss Parr said, `WHAT A LOVELY CLASS!´

TEACHER
I really have enjoyed the day.
Your work was good, and so was play.

THIS PLAY IS ALL ABOUT A RULE
WELL-KNOWN TO EVERYONE IN SCHOOL.

ALWAYS LISTEN WHEN IN CLASS,
AND TRY TO DO AS YOU ARE ASKED.

REPEAT SONG: HAPPY DAYS

If we all do as we´re asked ...

YEAH!

Performance Notes

Staging and performance tips (see stage plan)

- **Scene 1:** the story starts with a class of children engaged in typical classroom activities. Unless you have access to a bigger stage area, you will need to scale the larger items of play equipment down. For example, put the sand in a small plastic tray, and give the paint mixers three paint pots with brushes and the shop children two purses and a few goods to sell. The other items of equipment are small and can easily be put away in small containers in the clearing up scene.

- Miss Parr, the teacher, sits in her chair talking to a group of children looking at their work. Geraldine and Fred are in the Lego™ group and Melanie is in the book corner.

- After the introduction, allow a minute or two for the children to play before singing *A busy classroom*. During the song, the children only sing in those verses that describe what they're doing. Put the cleared up equipment around the sides of the stage.

- Scene 1 finishes with the children dejectedly moving to sit down on the floor, backs to the audience, facing their teacher.

- **Scene 2:** when the fire bell rings, the children leave the classroom centre front and line up in pairs, in the central aisle. Choose the children playing the parts of Amie West and Jack to lead off. Miss Parr walks along the line, checking names. Once Melanie has been tracked down, the children go back on stage and sit facing the teacher again. Amie West and Jack sit at the back of the class.

- **Scene 3:** The children stay in their positions to listen to the story.

Scenery

- Place a display board and a small, free-standing bookcase at the back of the performance area, with a teacher's chair in between. Cover the board with children's work relating to the assembly story, eg, Sun Safety or time.

Props

- Most of the props can be found in any KS1 classroom: a small tray for sand, books and cushions, painting aprons, pots of paint and brushes, items to sell and money for the shop, Lego™, beads and strings, a few toy cars, and boxes to store the small items of equipment.

- Miss Parr needs a large book or poster about Sun Safety, a class register and a storybook.

- The fire bell is heard off stage.

- You will also need a large clock to show the day progressing and then starting again. Either use a teaching clock or make a large clock out of strong card, using a PE hoop as a template. Draw round the outside of the hoop, cut out the circle and stick it to the hoop with tape. Write the hours on the clock face, and then fix the big and little clock hands firmly in the centre, using a large split pin. Allocate a child to move the clock hands round as the play progresses.

Costumes

- The children dress in whatever they usually wear to school.

Sound effects

- In the play, a cymbal roll heralds trouble. We hear it three times. Use a large suspended cymbal and encourage the player to make the roll using two soft beaters tapped on the rim of the cymbal. Start quietly and gradually get louder (crescendo). This will require practice.

- Rattle a wooden beater inside a large cowbell for the fire bell.

- Discuss with the children what magic music might sound like (eg, tinkling, quiet.) Experiment with pitched and unpitched chiming instruments (eg, wind chimes, jingles, wooden beaters rubbed gently over glockenspiel bars), and discuss whether the sounds you produce are effective. Put the sounds together into a magic music sequence, and choose a group of children to play it during the performance.

# Curriculum Links

Literacy Link
Stories with familiar settings.

# PSHE

Good listening

- In any discussion of this play, the focus should be on good listening, not misbehaviour. Why did the class miss their playtime? (Because Geraldine and Fred didn't listen to the teacher when she asked them to stop playing and clear up.)

- Young children often don't consider listening a priority because their own agenda is more urgent and interesting. Discuss with the children why they can't just do as they like in school. What would school be like if there was no adult in charge to teach, to remind, to encourage? Being a member of a class is like being a member of a sports team – why?

- Make listening a focus for a week or two. Introduce a magic sound, such as a quiet bell or jingles, to precede class announcements. (Don't use it too often.) Reward good listening.

What about me?

- A key theme of the story is not the misbehaviour of the four children, but the effects of this misbehaviour. Encourage the children to talk about the effect the behaviour of the four children in the story had on the teacher and the rest of the class.

Literacy

Rhyming couplets

- What do the children notice about the way this play is written? Read extracts from the play, leaving pauses at the end of the second lines so that the children can provide the missing rhyming words. Can they make up alternative second lines? For example:

    The children stopped, and, keen to please,
    Crawled around on hands and knees.

Maths

Time

- Talk about and record the key times in your school day, eg, start of school, morning play, lunchtime and home time. Look out for these times on the classroom clock. Use a clock with moving hands to work out how long various sessions last (eg, morning school, afternoon school, lunchtime, the whole school day).

The Awongalema Tree
by Kaye Umansky

Cast
Storyteller (adult)
Lion
Buffalo
Hare
Tiny Tortoise
Ants (about 12)
Mountain Spirit
Friends and relations of Hare and Buffalo (about 13 altogether)

Assembly theme

The Awongalema Tree describes the qualities of perseverance, modesty and courtesy.

Story

All the animals of the forest are starving. Hare, who prides herself on her speed, volunteers to run to the home of the Mountain Spirit and get the Magical Word that will make the Magic Tree produce delicious fruit. She arrives at the mountain and is given the Magical Word but, on her way back, trips over an anthill and, in the discomfort that ensues, forgets the word.

Buffalo and Lion are the next volunteers, but they are too wrapped up in themselves to learn from Hare's experience. They, too, crash into the anthill.

It is left to Tiny Tortoise to save the day. She isn't given a warm send-off, but plods off full of determination. She addresses the Mountain Spirit politely, is given the Magical Word, and begins the long journey home. She carefully skirts the anthill, and returns to the forest safely. Joyfully, the animals shout 'AWONGALEMA!', and the tree produces lots of wonderful fruit.

Setting

The setting for the play is a forest. The animal characters run between a forest clearing and Big Rock Mountain, home to the Mountain Spirit. In between the clearing and the mountain is a troublesome anthill.

Songs, chants and dances

There are two songs, both of which are repeated. *Mighty Mountain Spirit* is sung to the tune of *She'll be coming round the mountain*. *Go like the wind* is a chant. The play ends with a *Joyful dance*.

Script: The Awongalema Tree

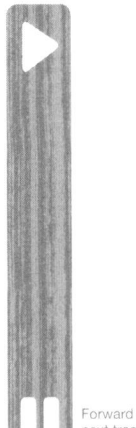

 **SONG: HUNGRY** *(Original)*

Hungry, so hungry,
Our tummies are empty.
Long weeks of sunshine
With no sign of rain.

Hungry, so hungry,
Our tummies are empty.
Send us some food
To fill them again.

Forward to next track

Once, there was a great famine, and all the animals in the forest were hungry. So hungry, their tummies hurt.

OHHHHHHH! (ACTION – RUB TUMMIES AND GROAN.)

There were no nuts to eat. No fruit growing. The trees had lost all their leaves. Even the grass was yellow and dry. Something had to be done.

They met at the foot of a tall tree growing in the middle of the forest.

(ACTION – ANIMALS GATHER AROUND THE TREE.)

Right now, it was bare, like all the others. But the legend was that this was a Magic Tree. If you called out a Special Magical Word it would grow wonderful, juicy, tasty fruit!

MMMMMMMM! (ACTION – ALL MOAN LONGINGLY.)

The problem was that it had been many years since the last famine and no-one knew the Word.

AHHHHHHH! (ACTION – SHAKE HEADS SADLY AND SIGH.)

Lion considered himself the animals' leader. The animals turned to him and said:

WHAT'S THE WORD, MR LION, WHAT'S THE WORD?

Lion thought and thought, then finally shook his head.
(ACTION – LION SHAKES HIS HEAD.)

He hated to admit it, but he just didn't know.

'But,' he said, 'there's a Wise Spirit who lives in a cave on Big Rock Mountain. One of us could go and ask it. The Spirit knows everything. Even more than me.'

'I'll go!' shouted Hare, jumping up eagerly.
(ACTION – JUMPS AROUND, HOLDING UP PAW.)

'Let me! I'm the fastest! Can I? Can I?'

'Very well,' said Lion. 'You can. And to help you on your way, your friends and relations will perform the *Good Luck Chant*.'

(ACTION – HARES FORM A RING AND LINK PAWS.)

CHANT: GO LIKE THE WIND (*Original*)

Go like the wind!
Fly like the bird!
Hurry on back
With the Magical Word! (x2)

Hare's friends and relations clapped her on the back, and everyone shouted:

GO, HARE, GO! (ACTION – ANIMALS CLAP HARE ON THE BACK.)

Hare went like the wind. (ACTION – HARE RUNS.)

SONG: MIGHTY MOUNTAIN SPIRIT
(*She'll be coming round the mountain*)

There's a mighty Mountain Spirit in a cave,
There's a mighty Mountain Spirit in a cave.
Go and tell it we're in trouble,
Then come back at the double,
And we'll clap you on the back for being brave!

When Hare reached the top of Big Rock Mountain, sure enough, there was a huge, dark cave. She took a deep breath and shouted in a high voice:

MOUNTAIN SPIRIT, SPEAK TO ME!
TELL ME THE NAME OF THE MAGIC TREE!

Everything went dark and scary. Thunder rolled. (SOUND EFFECT.)
And a great, booming voice called out:

AWONGALEMA!

'Got it!' said Hare. 'Awongalema. I must remember that.'

And she raced recklessly back down the mountain.
But she was going so fast that she ran straight into a huge ant hill!

CRASH! (SOUND EFFECT – CYMBAL CRASH.)

All the ants went scurrying everywhere! Hare wriggled and giggled, they tickled so much! (ACTION – ANTS TICKLE HARE.)

TEE-HEE-HEE! (ACTION – HARE GIGGLES AND SQUIRMS.)

Hare finally managed to escape. Still giggling, she brushed off the ants still clinging to her fur.

When she arrived back in the forest, the animals all shouted:

WHAT'S THE WORD, MRS HARE, WHAT'S THE WORD?

Hare said in a guilty voice:

I'M FEELING REALLY ROTTEN,
BUT I THINK I HAVE FORGOTTEN.

And the hungry animals said:

OHHHHHHH ... (ACTION – DROOP SADLY AND RUB TUMMIES.)

 REPEAT SONG: **HUNGRY**

Hungry, so hungry ...

Forward to
next track

 *Script* – THE AWONGALEMA TREE   CLASS ASSEMBLIES © 2010 A&C Black Publishers Ltd

'I'll go,' said Buffalo. 'You need muscle for a mission like this.'
(ACTION – BUFFALO STRIDES AROUND FLEXING BICEPS.)

'Very well,' agreed Lion. 'Buffalo's friends and relations, please take your places for the *Good Luck Chant*.'

(ACTION – BUFFALOES FORM A RING AND LINK HOOVES.)

REPEAT CHANT: **GO LIKE THE WIND**

Go like the wind ...

Buffalo's supporters clapped him on the back and shouted:

GO, BUFFALO, GO!

The ground shook as Buffalo galloped off, snorting.
(ACTION – BUFFALO RUNS.)

REPEAT SONG: **MIGHTY MOUNTAIN SPIRIT**

There's a mighty Mountain Spirit in a cave ...

When Buffalo reached the Mountain Spirit's cave, he pawed the ground and shouted in a deep, gruff voice:

MOUNTAIN SPIRIT, SPEAK TO ME!
TELL ME THE NAME OF THE MAGIC TREE!

Again, all went dark and thunder rolled. (SOUND EFFECT.)

Then the voice boomed:

AWONGALEMA!

'Aha!' said Buffalo. 'Awongalema. I must remember that.'

And he lumbered off back down the mountain. But ... oh dear. He wasn't looking where he was going, and charged straight into that ant hill!

CRASH! (SOUND EFFECT – CYMBAL CRASH.)

All the ants went swarming around again! They were a bit cross this time, and gave Buffalo some nasty little pinches through his thick fur.
(ACTION – ANTS PINCH BUFFALO.)

OW! OW! OW! (ACTION – BUFFALO LEAPS AROUND, BATTING AT THE ANTS.)

Those ants hurt! Buffalo pushed and shoved his way out of the ants. He was covered in bruises.

When he arrived back in the forest, the animals all shouted:

WHAT'S THE WORD, MR BUFFALO, WHAT'S THE WORD?

And Buffalo had to confess the truth. He said:

I'M FEELING REALLY ROTTEN, BUT I THINK I HAVE FORGOTTEN.

And the hungry animals said:

OHHHHHHH ... (ACTION – DROOP AND RUB TUMMIES.)

REPEAT SONG: HUNGRY

Hungry, so hungry ...

'None of you can be trusted,' sighed Lion. 'I'll just have to go myself. Don't worry about the chant, I shan't need it.'

Hare and Buffalo clapped Lion on the back and shouted:

GO, LION, GO!

Off stalked Lion, swishing his tail and looking confident.
(ACTION – LION STALKS OFF.)

REPEAT SONG: MIGHTY MOUNTAIN SPIRIT

There's a mighty Mountain Spirit in a cave ...

When Lion reached the Mountain Spirit's cave, he shouted in a commanding voice:

MOUNTAIN SPIRIT, SPEAK TO ME!
TELL ME THE NAME OF THE MAGIC TREE!

Everything went dark and thunder rolled. (SOUND EFFECT.)
And once again, the voice boomed:

AWONGALEMA!

'So that's it,' said Lion. 'Awongalema. Of course, I knew I'd be the one
to get it right.'

Off he went, back down the mountain, with his nose in the air – but this
meant that he didn't see the ant hill.

CRASH! (SOUND EFFECT – CYMBAL CRASH.)

For the third time, the ant's home had been destroyed. They were
furious! They swarmed all over Lion, biting really hard! (ACTION – ANTS
ATTACK LION.)

OWWWWWWWW! (LION LEAPS AROUND, BATTING AT THE ANTS.)

Slapping at the angry ants, Lion stalked away.

When he arrived back in the forest, the animals all shouted:

WHAT'S THE WORD, MR LION, WHAT'S THE WORD?

Lion wasn't so proud now. He stared at his ant-chewed tail and said:

I'M FEELING REALLY ROTTEN,
BUT I THINK I HAVE FORGOTTEN.

And the hungry animals said:

OHHHHHHH ... (ACTION – DROOP SADLY AND RUB TUMMIES.)

They were so sad. If even Lion couldn't remember the Magical Word,
it seemed that all was lost. But then, a small, timid voice said:

MAY I TRY? (ACTION – TINY TORTOISE MOVES FORWARD.)

The voice belonged to Tiny Tortoise. Nobody had even noticed that she was there. The animals nudged each other and laughed behind their paws. (ACTION – LAUGHTER AND NUDGING.)

'Don't be silly,' said Hare. 'You're not speedy.'

'Or strong,' said Buffalo.

'Or clever,' added Lion.

'I'd still like to try,' said Tiny Tortoise.

'Suit yourself,' said Lion with a shrug. 'But you'll never make it.'

Nobody suggested the *Good Luck Chant*. Tiny Tortoise didn't have any relations and was too shy to make friends. Everyone just sighed and turned away. (ACTION – ANIMALS TURN AWAY.)

But Tiny Tortoise set off anyway. (ACTION – TINY TORTOISE STARTS WALKING SLOWLY TOWARDS BIG ROCK MOUNTAIN.)

It took a long, long time to get to the top of Big Rock Mountain. The sun was setting when she finally arrived at the cave. She was so, so tired. But she used the last of her breath to call out in a shy little voice:

MOUNTAIN SPIRIT, SPEAK TO ME!
TELL ME THE NAME OF THE MAGIC TREE ...

... PLEASE?

Did you notice that extra little word?

This time, there was no thunder. It all went very quiet. And then the voice said:

AWONGALEMA!

'Thank you,' said Tiny Tortoise. 'Awongalema. I shall remember that.'

And she crawled off back down the slope, saying the Magical Word over and over again with each slow, small step. (ACTION – TINY TORTOISE BEGINS WALKING.)

AWONGALEMA – AWONGALEMA – AWONGALEMA ...

She saw the ant hill, and carefully walked round it, still repeating the Word.

AWONGALEMA — AWONGALEMA — AWONGALEMA ...

The ants were very relieved.

When she arrived back in the forest, the animals all shouted:

WHAT'S THE WORD, TINY TORTOISE, WHAT'S THE WORD?

And Tiny Tortoise said:

AWONGALEMA. (TORTOISE ONLY.)

'That's it!' cried Hare, Buffalo and Lion. 'Awongalema!'

And everyone jumped to their feet and shouted:

AWONGALEMA!

And the Magic Tree burst forth with the most wonderful fruit you could ever imagine! (SOUND AND ACTION.)

All the animals fell upon the fruit and ate and ate and ate until they were full to bursting! (ACTION – ANIMALS MIME EATING FRUIT.)

Then they danced around the tree under a big, yellow moon. The famine was finally over – and they were so happy. But Tiny Tortoise was happiest of all.

MUSIC: **JOYFUL DANCE** (*Original*)

Performance Notes

Staging and performance tips (see stage plan)

- *The Awongalema Tree* involves a lot of movement between the forest glade where the animals are gathered and the cave of the Mountain Spirit in Big Rock Mountain. In between the two is an anthill. Place the mountain away from the main performance area. The anthill is also off stage, to the left, right or centre of the main performance area.

- At the appropriate moment in the story, the ants form an anthill shape by huddling together facing inwards, arms wrapped round each other. On being disturbed, they break away from each other and swarm all over the clumsy animals before reforming their anthill shape.

Scenery

- Use PE equipment and drapes to build the mountain and cave. A few steps at the foot of the mountain would give the audience a good view of Hare, Buffalo, Lion and Tortoise as they climb up to the cave.

- The centrepiece of the forest glade is the Magic Tree. Make a strong roll of corrugated card for the trunk and smaller rolls for three or four branches. Cut lots of pieces of exotic fruit out of strong card, paint one side in a bright colour, and sprinkle with glitter. When they are dry, do the same to the other side. Attach about half the fruit to the branches and put the rest around the base of the tree. Support the tree on a rounders hurdle.

- Give the tree a parched appearance by draping it with thin, smooth, brown or grey fabric such as gauze, or a silky sari length, making sure the fruit on the floor is covered. When the Magical Word is finally pronounced, a couple of the children uncover the fruit at the base of the tree and distribute it to the hungry animals. Stand a few smaller, leafless trees at the back of the stage.

- Make a forest backdrop: paint or print an abstract mixture of tree trunks, branches, leaves, ferns and fronds in various shades of green and brown. Mount on a freestanding display board and place at the back of the stage. Twist several long strips of green, yellow and brown crepe paper together to make creepers, and hang across the top of the trees.

☼ Costumes

- **Lion:** dress Lion in a plain yellow or brown long-sleeved top and trousers or tights. Make a hairy chest by attaching a bib made of fur fabric to the front of the top. Wear brown socks over hands for paws. Plait brown tights to make a tail. Fray the ends and paint black. Attach furry ears to a headband. For the mane, cut a large oval shape out of card and make a hole in the middle for the actor's head to go through. Paint the mane dark brown then stick fur fabric all over it on both sides.

- **Hares:** plain white, long-sleeved tops and tights or trousers. Put white or black socks over hands, and make fluffy tails out of white fur fabric. Attach long, furry white ears with brown insides to headbands.

- **Buffaloes:** the buffaloes wear black. Attach long, curved horns to headbands, and stick a tuft of black fur in between the horns. Wear black socks over hands and shiny black shoes. Make short tails by plaiting black tights together and fraying the ends.

- **Tiny Tortoise:** Tiny Tortoise wears a dark brown long-sleeved top and trousers. Use a large, oval cardboard serving dish for the shell (the sort used by catering companies). Paint it brown and add tortoiseshell markings. Punch holes in the shell and attach elastic loops to fit over the shoulders and round the waist. You could add a headdress: sketch and decorate a small, beaky tortoise head with black, beady eyes and attach to a cardboard headband.

- **Ants:** the ants wear black plimsolls, tights and long-sleeved tops. Either cut ant heads out of card and attach to headbands, or stick two ant eyes to a headband and add two pipe cleaner antennae.

- **Mountain Spirit:** the Mountain Spirit can pop out of the cave to say the Magical Word. Dress the spirit in black and attach strips of grey, white, black and red crepe paper or ribbon to the front, back and arms of the costume. A black balaclava will complete the spooky appearance.

☼ Sound effects

- **Mountain Spirit:** experiment to find thunder sounds. (Wobbling a large piece of stiff card is tricky but effective.) Choose a child with a deep, loud voice to say 'AWONGALEMA!' Cup hands over mouth to produce an echoing sound. Use a microphone for dramatic effect.

- Use a cymbal roll followed by a crash each time the animals run into the anthill.

Curriculum Links

PSHE

- Why were Lion, Hare and Buffalo so sure they would succeed in bringing the Magical Word back to the animals? Why were the animals surprised when Tortoise volunteered her services? What do you think about the animals' refusal to perform the *Good Luck Chant* for Tortoise?

- Tortoise wasn't fast, strong or a clever leader, but she was the only animal that succeeded in remembering the Magical Word. Why?

Concentration

- Why did Hare, Buffalo and Lion run into the anthill? Why did they forget the Magical Word? Why is it sometimes difficult to concentrate in class? (Eg, noisy play and chattering, thoughts keep coming into heads, other pupils chatting or fidgeting.)

Courtesy

- Why was there no thunder when Tortoise asked for the Magical Word?

Science

- Water is essential for plant growth. People need fruits, seeds and vegetables to live. Some countries don't have a lot of rain and this can lead to famine. In our country we usually have enough rain, but sometimes, in hot weather, we have to use water more carefully.

- How can we save water? (Eg, shower rather than have a bath, don't leave the tap running when cleaning teeth or washing dishes.)

Music

- Clap these words as you chant them:
  Ma-gic Tree (three claps)
  Mi-ghty Moun-tain Spi-rit (six claps, to the same rhythm as *Ring-a-ring-a-ro-ses*)
  Big Rock Moun-tain (four claps)
  Repeat each chant at least four times.

- Make up two-note tunes for these chants, using two chime bars (E and G). Leave the chimes out so the children can experiment with them.

The Enormous Turnip
by Pippa Goodhart

Cast
Storyteller (adult)
Little old man
Little old lady
Kind neighbour, girl and boy from next door
Dog, cat and mouse
Dancing butterflies (about 10)
Villagers (about 10)

The eight central characters have small speaking parts.

Assembly theme
This version of a traditional tale focuses on problem-solving and team work.

Story
The little old lady and her husband have no food or money, and their cottage is falling down. The little old man gives in to despair, but his wife comes up with some original solutions to their problems. Her secret weapon is the enormous turnip growing in their garden. Her plan is to pull up the turnip, make the middle into soup, and then use the tough shell for a new home.

The problem is that the turnip seems reluctant to leave the vegetable patch. Watched by a curious group of locals, a grand total of five people and three animals tug at the stubborn vegetable. It's a mouse's sneeze that finally tips the balance, and out pops the turnip.

The little old lady doesn't waste any time. She sets about making soup, and invites everyone to share it. The neighbours and the animals provide all sorts of tasty ingredients for the soup pot, while the little old man starts converting the turnip shell into a cosy little house.

Setting
The setting is the tumbledown house and garden of an elderly couple. The tale has an old-fashioned feel, which is reflected in the scenery and costumes.

Songs and chants
The three songs are simple – two are set to familiar tunes. There are opportunities for all the children to join in repeated chants and vocal sound effects.

Script: The Enormous Turnip

Scene 1: No food, no money, no home

STORYTELLER

There was once a little old lady and a little old man, who lived in a little old cottage. They were very happy together, but they had nothing to eat in their cupboard, and their cottage was so old that it was falling down.

LITTLE OLD MAN

We haven't got anything to eat.

NO FOOD! (ACTION – RUB TUMMIES.)

LITTLE OLD MAN

We haven't got any money.

NO MONEY! (ACTION – TURN POCKETS OUT.)

LITTLE OLD MAN

And our cottage is falling down!

NO HOME! (ACTION – SHIVER AND SHAKE.)

STORYTELLER

'Whatever shall we do?' asked the little old man. He sat down on his chair and gave in to despair.

'You give up too easily, that's your trouble,' said the little old lady. 'We'll build ourselves a new house.'

'We haven't got anything to build a house out of!' said the little old man. 'You can't make a house out of nothing!'

But the little old lady didn't let a problem like that put her off. 'It's no good thinking about what we haven't got. Let's think about what we *have* got,' she said.

'But what have we got?' said the little old man.

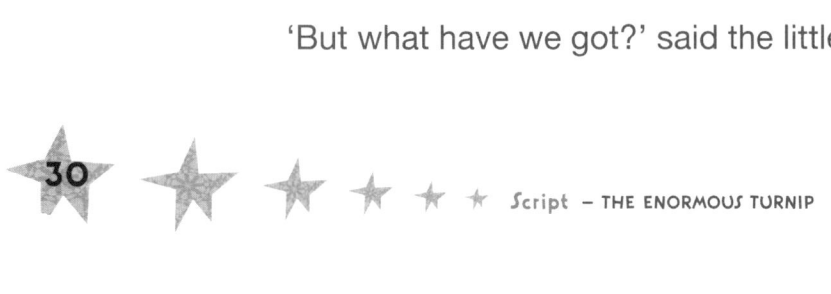

Script – THE ENORMOUS TURNIP

The little old lady smiled and said:

LITTLE OLD LADY
Follow me and you will see.

STORYTELLER
The little old lady and the little old man went out into the garden.

(ACTION – WALK INTO GARDEN. LITTLE OLD MAN POKES THE GROUND WITH A STICK.)

They found one wizened carrot and a few small potatoes. And …

(SOUND EFFECT – CYMBAL ROLL AND CRASH.)

Something big and round and purple was growing out of the ground. It was a turnip! But it wasn't just any old turnip. It was a ...

A GREAT BIG ENORMOUS TURNIP!
(ACTION – DRAW HUGE CIRCLES IN THE AIR WITH ARMS.)

Forward to next track

SONG: I'M A GREAT BIG TURNIP (*I'm a little teapot*)

I'm a great big turnip,
Fat and round.
See me growing
In the ground.

When I've finished growing,
Give a shout!
Make some soup
And pour it out.

MMMMM! SLURP! YUMMY!
(ACTION – MIME EATING SOUP.)

'We can eat that for a good few meals,' said the little old man.
'It'll make a delicious soup!'

'We can do better than that,' said the little old lady. 'It's big enough to live in too – if only we can pull it out of the ground.'

REPEAT SONG: I'M A GREAT BIG TURNIP

I'm a great big turnip ...

... Cut a door
And scoop me out!

MMMM, COSY! (ACTION – WRAP ARMS AROUND CHEST AND SNUGGLE.)

Scene 2: Heave ho!

So the little old lady and the little old man took hold of the turnip's leaves, and they pulled. (ACTION – PULL.)

CHANT: HEAVE HO! (*Original*)

Heave ho! Heave ho!
Whatever you do, don't let go.
Nice and easy, nice and slow,
Heave ho! Heave ho!

... but the turnip wouldn't move!

WE PULL AND PULL WITH ALL OUR MIGHT, BUT STILL THAT TURNIP HOLDS ON TIGHT!

A kind neighbour and his two children saw what was happening. The neighbour called out:

NEIGHBOUR
Do you need any help?

LITTLE OLD LADY AND LITTLE OLD MAN
Yes please! (ACTION – NOD HEADS.)

STORYTELLER
So the neighbour held onto the little old man, who held onto the little old lady.

Together they pulled and pulled ... (ACTION – ALL PULL.)

REPEAT CHANT: HEAVE HO!

Heave ho! Heave ho ...

Script – THE ENORMOUS TURNIP

… but still the turnip would not move!

WE PULL AND PULL WITH ALL OUR MIGHT, BUT STILL THAT TURNIP HOLDS ON TIGHT!

'Come and help us, children!' called the neighbour. So the boy and the girl came running over from next door and grabbed hold of the neighbour, who held onto the little old man, who held onto the little old lady.

Together they pulled and pulled … (ACTION – ALL PULL.)

REPEAT CHANT: HEAVE HO!

Heave ho! Heave ho …

Forward to next track

… but that turnip just would not move at all!

WE PULL AND PULL WITH ALL OUR MIGHT, BUT STILL THAT TURNIP HOLDS ON TIGHT!

Well, by now the little old man was hot and cross. 'There's nobody left to help,' he said. 'We'll have to give up now!'

'Nonsense!' cried the little old lady. 'There's always something else you can try! We can't give up now. Think, everyone!'
(ACTION – ALL LOOK THOUGHTFUL.)

DOG
Woof, woof, woof!
(ACTION – DOG TUGS THE LITTLE OLD LADY'S SKIRT.)

STORYTELLER
'The dog will help us, won't you, dog?' said the little old lady.
(ACTION – DOG NODS.)

So the dog grabbed hold of the girl, who held onto her brother, who held onto the neighbour, who held onto the little old man, who held onto the little old lady.

Together they pulled and pulled … (ACTION – ALL PULL.)

REPEAT CHANT: HEAVE HO!

Heave ho! Heave ho …

Forward to next track

… but still no luck.

WE PULL AND PULL WITH ALL OUR MIGHT, BUT STILL THAT TURNIP HOLDS ON TIGHT!

'Well, that's it, isn't it?' said the little old man. 'There's one, two, three, four, five, six of us pulling, and it still won't come up! We'll have to give up after all!'

'I'm not giving up!' said the little old lady. 'There are always more ways to try!'

CAT
Miaow! (ACTION – CAT LICKS PAWS AND WASHES EARS.)

STORYTELLER
'Thank you, cat,' said the little old lady. So the cat grabbed hold of the dog, who held onto the girl, who held onto her brother, who held onto the neighbour, who held onto the little old man, who held onto the little old lady.

Together they pulled and pulled … (ACTION – ALL PULL.)

REPEAT CHANT: HEAVE HO!

Heave ho! Heave ho …

… but nothing moved – nothing at all.

WE PULL AND PULL WITH ALL OUR MIGHT, BUT STILL THAT TURNIP HOLDS ON TIGHT!

Well, by now, even the little old lady was getting a bit worried. But she was never one to give up. Looking around for inspiration, she caught the eye of a little mouse, who was watching with interest.

MOUSE
Squeak!
(ACTION – MOUSE CROUCHES DOWN AND TWITCHES WHISKERS.)

'Yes please, mouse! You pull too!' said the little old lady.

So the mouse grabbed hold of the cat, who held onto the dog, who held onto the girl, who held onto her brother, who held onto the neighbour, who held onto the little old man, who held onto the little old lady.

Together they pulled and pulled … (ACTION – ALL PULL.)

REPEAT CHANT: HEAVE HO!

Heave ho! Heave ho …

… and pulled and pulled, but the turnip held firm. Oh dear! It really did seem that nothing would ever move that great big enormous turnip. But, just then …

(ACTION – BUTTERFLIES FLUTTER BY.)

Some butterflies came flying and swooping past.

MUSIC: BUTTERFLY DANCE (*Original*)

The tiny breeze from the butterflies' wings was just enough to make the mouse sneeze.

MOUSE
Atishoo! (ACTION – SNEEZE.)

STORYTELLER
And that made all the difference! The mouse jerked backwards, giving a sharp tug on the cat's tail. The cat yowled and pulled the dog, who pulled the girl, who pulled her brother, who pulled the neighbour, who pulled the little old man, who pulled the little old lady, who pulled the turnip …

POP! (SOUND EFFECT – LOUD TAP ON A LARGE TAMBOUR.)

And out came the great big enormous turnip! Down tumbled the mouse and the cat and the dog and the girl and the boy and the neighbour and the little old man and the little old lady.

WHOOAAHH! (ACTION – ALL FALL BACKWARDS.)

Scene 3: Turnip Soup

The little old lady landed quite comfortably on top of the pile. Up she jumped, quick as a flash!

'Now,' she said. 'I'm going to cut a hole in the side of that turnip and chop out the insides and make a good soup. Anybody who brings something to add to the soup is welcome to share it.'

(ACTION – THE LITTLE OLD LADY CUTS UP THE TURNIP.)

HURRAH! (ACTION – PUNCH FISTS IN AIR.)

Everyone scrambled to their feet and scurried off to find ingredients to add to the soup. (ACTION.)

Soon they were back, and so were all their friends!

NEIGHBOUR, BOY AND GIRL
We've brought some onions.

DOG
I've brought some flour.

CAT
I've brought some garlic.

MOUSE
And I've brought some salt and pepper.
(ACTION – EVERYONE PUTS THEIR OFFERINGS IN THE COOKING POT.)

CROWD
And we've all brought bowls and spoons!
(ACTION – EVERYONE HOLDS UP THEIR BOWLS AND SPOONS.)

STORYTELLER
'Good,' said the little old lady. She turned to her husband. 'Little old husband, you turn that turnip shell into a cosy little house, while I make the soup.'

'Righto, dear,' said the little old man. And he set to work.

(ACTION – THE LITTLE OLD MAN DRAGS THE TURNIP IN FRONT OF THE BACKDROP AND STARTS TO CARVE OUT A HOUSE. THE LITTLE OLD LADY STIRS THE SOUP. EVERYONE ELSE WAITS, THEIR BOWLS AT THE READY.)

Soon the smell of the good soup filled the air.

MMMMMM!

The little old lady ladled out the soup. (ACTION.) There was enough for everyone.

DELICIOUS!

Script – THE ENORMOUS TURNIP

Soon the party turned into a house warming party, because the turnip made a very nice house indeed for the little old man and the little old lady to live in.

'Thank you, everyone, for all your help!' the little old man and the little old lady called out.

LITTLE OLD MAN AND LITTLE OLD LADY
Thank you, everyone!

CROWD
You're welcome!

SONG: **LITTLE HOUSE** (*Shiny little house*)

We're glad, very glad,
That we have a little house,
We've got room for our friends,
And the dog and cat and mouse.

And it's fit for a king,
And it's fit for a queen,
It's the nicest little turnip house
We've ever seen.

Performance Notes

Staging and performance tips (see stage plan)

- At the start of the play, the kind neighbour and his two children stand behind the fence. The villagers and the butterflies wait off-stage – they can sit on benches or chairs. They join in the chants and songs and generally provide encouragement. As the drama develops, the villagers, in twos and threes, come on stage and watch the proceedings from behind the fence.

- Place the turnip off-stage on the right, near the front. Cover it with a brown drape, leaving the top showing. Hide someone under the drape to hold the turnip in place.

- **Scene 1:** the play starts with the old couple standing at the back of the stage, bemoaning their fate. They walk along the front of the stage from left to right, looking for something to eat in their vegetable patch.

- **Scene 2:** the line of people and animals pulling the turnip goes across the stage from right to left. Remind the children to *pretend* to pull the turnip.

- The butterflies flutter onto the main stage area from stage right. They dance around the line of people and animals and leave the stage front left. They settle either on the floor in front of the stage, or in their starting positions.

- After the 'POP', the person holding the turnip pushes it onto the main stage area and everyone falls over. The little old lady and her husband pick themselves up and move to their starting positions at the back. The rest of the characters stay on the floor until invited to find ingredients.

- **Scene 4:** the little old lady mimes cutting up the turnip. The turnip-pullers exit, stage left, to fetch their contributions. They run back on stage, drop them into the cooking pot and sit down in a line along the front of the stage, backs to the audience. The villagers, still behind the fence, produce bowls and spoons. While the little old lady is dishing up the soup, the turnip is removed, and the board is turned round to show the turnip house.

Scenery

- Paint a tumble down cottage, and mount on a freestanding display board. On the other side of the board, mount a picture of a turnip house. Put the board at the back of the stage on the right, with the picture of the old cottage facing the audience.

Teaching Notes – THE ENORMOUS TURNIP

- Use long strips of waist-high corrugated card for the picket fence. Paint a sturdy post at each end, and white horizontal slats (with pointed tops) along the length. Attach the card fence to three or four PE posts. (Alternatively, tie a rope between PE supports.)

Props

- Cover a large ball or space-hopper with a white or purple cloth. Tie the fabric securely at the pulling end, leaving enough material for the little old lady to get hold of. If you are using a spacehopper, leave the rubber handles uncovered.

- Additional props: two stools, a wizened carrot and a few shrivelled potatoes, two big play knives, a large cooking pot, soup ladle, flour, garlic, salt and pepper, bowls and spoons for everyone.

Costumes

- **Villagers:** the village women and girls wear long-sleeved white blouses, long or knee-length skirts, tights and sturdy shoes. The women wear shawls and the girls wear headscarves. The little old lady has her sleeves rolled up and wears an apron. The village men wear plain or check long-sleeved shirts, long or knee-length trousers held up with belts or string, and sturdy shoes. The little old man carries a stick.

- **Dog, cat and mouse:** plain, long-sleeved top, tights or trousers, and plimsolls. Attach a white fur bib to the cat's and the mouse's tops. Make tails out stuffed fur fabric for the dog and cat, and paint a length of thin rope pink for the mouse's tail. Attach fabric dog, cat and mouse ears to headbands.

- **Butterflies:** the butterflies wear brightly coloured tights and tops. Cut symmetrical wings out of card and fold down the middle. Paint one side with thick paint, then fold the other side on top of it to make a mirror image pattern. Attach to shoulders and waist with tape or elastic. Fix pipe cleaner antennae to headbands.

Sound effects

- Experiment with soundmakers to produce the following sound effects:
  NO FOOD! Roll large stones around in a shoebox (rumbling tummies).
  NO MONEY! Jingle some coins in a bag.
  NO HOME! Tip some wooden bricks on the floor.
  POP! Tap loudly on a large tambour.

Curriculum Links

Literacy Link
Traditional and fairy tales.

PSHE

Positive and negative thinking

- How do you think the little old man feels when he realises that there is no food or money, and his house is falling down? Pretend to be the little old man and say, 'Whatever shall we do?' Think about how he might stand and sit. What sort of expression would he have on his face? What sort of voice would he use?

- The little old lady says, 'It's no good thinking about what we haven't got. Let's think about what we have got.' What does she mean? Pretend to be the little old lady and say, 'We'll build ourselves a new house.' Think about how she might stand and sit. What sort of expression would she have on her face? What sort of voice would she use?

ACTIVITY BOX: LET'S LOOK ON THE BRIGHT SIDE

Tell the children you are going to pretend to be like the little old man. Make up a bad luck story, eg 'My model has collapsed and I'll never be able to make it again'. Speak in a miserable voice. Ask the children to think what the little old lady might have replied to this statement. Encourage the children to stand up straight and use a cheerful voice.

Team work

- Getting the turnip out of the ground needed a team of eight pullers and a sneeze. Which lesson-related jobs need a group of people to get them done quickly and well? (Eg, getting out and putting away PE equipment, clearing up after a play session.)

- Choose a few children to go off in pairs and find out what other school jobs are done by a team. They could watch the hall being set up for school lunch, interview the caretaker about cleaning the school, or talk to members of the office staff about producing the school newsletter.

Superstars on Mars
by Jenny McLachlan

Cast

Storyteller (adult)
Robots (about 5), including the captain of the spaceship, Rocky and Robyn
Aliens (about 8), including Arno, Astra, Aggie and Alina
Moon monkeys (about 6), including Malvena
Stars (about 11), including Stella

The named members of the cast have short speaking parts.

Assembly theme

Superstars on Mars shows that everyone has useful skills, and that a range of talents, however unspectacular they may seem to those who possess them, is needed for good teamwork.

Story

Spacebuster 1001, with a cargo of alien tourists, is returning from a day out on the moon. Despite the efforts of the captain and his robot crew, it flies into a storm of asteroids and crashes into the red dust of Mars.

There are several problems facing the travellers. However, the robots manage to mend the hole in the spaceship, the moon monkeys bounce around to jerk the spaceship out of the crater, and the stars solve the lighting problem.

But what have the aliens contributed to this rescue mission? They feel very dejected when they contemplate their apparent uselessness, until it is pointed out that it was they who came up with all the good ideas, and it was they who provided the encouragement and praise necessary to spur the others to action.

Setting

The scene is Mars – a desolate place with rocks and red dust, but home to the amiable moon monkeys.

Songs

There are four songs, three of which are set to traditional tunes. The first, *We're stuck on Mars*, is repeated several times and is adapted to provide a positive finale. Encourage the children to use their character voices in the songs.

Script: Superstars on Mars

Scene 1: Big trouble

STORYTELLER

Over the stars and far, far away, a spaceship was in trouble. *Big* trouble.

'This is your captain speaking,' came a voice from the speakers in the ceiling.

The aliens on board Spacebuster 1001 glanced at each other nervously. (ACTION.) They had just had a wonderful day out on the moon, and now they were on their way home. The journey had been going well until ... just as they were navigating the tricky airspace around Mars, the spaceship entered a cloud of asteroids.

As the captain of the spaceship attempted to steer a path through the asteroids, the aliens and the crew of robots were bumped and bounced about in their seats. (ACTION – ALL BOUNCE IN SEATS.)

WHOAH! (ACTION – ALL HOLD HEADS AND LOOK SCARED.)

'Fasten your seatbelts!' came the captain's voice.

The robot crew tried hard to keep their balance as they helped the aliens with their seatbelts. (ACTION – ROBOTS HELP ALIENS.)

'Put down your moon juice: we are making an emergency landing on Mars!'

CRASH! BANG! WALLOP!

The Spacebuster shot through the atmosphere of Mars and landed, with a massive crash, in a crater.

When they had got their breath back and checked for broken bones, the helpful crew of robots guided the aliens out of the battered spaceship. (ACTION.)

Standing in the red dust of Mars, the aliens beeped and wiggled their fingers nervously. (ACTION AND ALIEN SOUND EFFECTS.)

Everyone gazed at the Spacebuster – and the big hole that had appeared in it.

ALIENS

What are we going to do?

ROBOTS

How are we going to get home?

 **SONG: WE'RE STUCK ON MARS** (*Original*)

(ALIENS)

We fell through the sky,
And crashed with a THUMP! (ACTION – JOLT ON 'THUMP'.)
(ROBOTS)
Our spaceship is broken,
And we've got the hump. (ACTION – SLUMP SHOULDERS.)
(ALIENS)
Please can you help us? (ACTION – TURN TO ROBOTS.)
(ROBOTS)
We haven't a clue! (ACTION – SHAKE HEADS.)
(ALIENS + ROBOTS)
We're stuck on Mars and there's nothing we can do!
(ACTION – FACE AUDIENCE, WIGGLING FINGERS AND PRESSING
BUTTONS.)

Forward to
next track

STORYTELLER

'Hang on,' said the captain. 'What's that chattering noise?'

Squinting through the dust, the robots and aliens caught sight of several
pairs of eyes peering at them. All of a sudden, a group of strange
creatures leapt from behind the rocks.
(ACTION – MONKEYS BOUNCE AND JUMP.)

MALVENA THE MONKEY

I'm Malvena, and we're the moon monkeys. How are you going to fix
that? (ACTION – POINTS TO HOLE.)

 **REPEAT SONG: WE'RE STUCK ON MARS**

We fell through the sky ...

Forward to
next track

Scene 2: Grab a tool

STORYTELLER
But then, Arno the Alien had a great idea.

ARNO THE ALIEN
Wait a minute. Robots are good at mending each other. Maybe they can mend spaceships too!

SONG: IF YOU'RE HANDY AND YOU KNOW IT
(*If you're happy and you know it*)

If you're handy and you know it,
Grab a tool.
If you're handy and you know it,
Grab a tool.
If you're handy and you know it,
And you really want to show it,
If you're handy and you know it,
Grab a tool.

Forward to next track

(ACTION – DURING THE SONG, THE ROBOTS SET ABOUT REPAIRING THE HOLE IN THE SPACESHIP.)

STORYTELLER
In no time at all, the robots had fixed the hole in the spaceship.

The aliens beeped and wiggled their fingers with delight.
(ACTION AND SOUND.)

ALIENS
You're fantastic! You're amazing!
You are the superstars on Mars!

STORYTELLER
The robots felt so proud of themselves that they pressed their buttons and whirred like crazy! (ACTION AND SOUND.)

But Rocky the Robot wasn't as excited as the others. He was staring into the crater where the Spacebuster had crash-landed.

He called out, 'We still can't go home. How will we get the spaceship out of the crater?'

 Script – SUPERSTARS ON MARS

REPEAT SONG: WE´RE STUCK ON MARS

We fell through the sky ...

Forward to
next track

Scene 3: Everywhere a jump, jump!

But then, Astra the Alien had a great idea.

ASTRA THE ALIEN
Wait a minute. The moon monkeys are good at jumping. Maybe they can bounce us out of this hole!

SONG: JUMP, JUMP *(Old MacDonald)*

(ALIENS AND ROBOTS)
These moon monkeys, they can jump,
Ee-i ee-i oh. (ACTION – JUMP THREE TIMES.)
They´ll move this spaceship with a thump,
Ee-i ee-i oh. (ACTION – JUMP THREE TIMES.)
With a great jump here,
And a great jump there.
Here a jump,
There a jump,
Everywhere a jump, jump.
These moon monkeys, they can jump,
Ee-i ee-i oh. (ACTION – JUMP THREE TIMES.)

Forward to
next track

(ACTION – DURING THE SONG, THE MONKEYS JUMP AND MOVE THE SPACESHIP OUT OF THE CRATER.)

STORYTELLER
The moon monkeys jumped and jumped until the spaceship popped out of the crater and came to rest on flat ground.

The aliens beeped and wiggled their fingers with delight.
(ACTION AND SOUND.)

ALIENS
You're fantastic! You're amazing!
You are the superstars on Mars!

STORYTELLER

The moon monkeys felt so proud of themselves that they grinned and bounced around all over the place. (ACTION – MONKEYS BOUNCE.)

Happy to be going home at last, the aliens and robots headed towards the spaceship.

But just as they got to the door, Robyn the Robot stopped them.

ROBYN THE ROBOT

Our lights are broken! How can we take off into space without lights?

REPEAT SONG: WE'RE STUCK ON MARS

We fell through the sky ...

Forward to next track

Scene 4: Stars shining bright

STORYTELLER

The aliens, robots and moon monkeys all sat down in the red dust of Mars and put their heads in their hands. (ACTION – HEADS IN HANDS.)

All of a sudden, far, far above them, a constellation of twinkling, shimmering stars began to move and dance.

(ACTION – ALIENS AND ROBOTS SHIELD THEIR EYES AS THE STARS TWINKLE AND DANCE.)

SONG: STARS SHINING BRIGHT

(*Kite flying high in the blue of the sky*)

**Stars shining bright in the darkness of space.
Shine, shine and glow we go,
Shine, shine and glow we go,
Shine, shine and glow we go,
Twinkling with grace.**

Forward to next track

AGGIE THE ALIEN

Wait a minute. The stars are great at shining. Maybe they could light our way home!

STELLA THE STAR

I'm Stella the Star. We'd love to help you.

  Script – SUPERSTARS ON MARS   CLASS ASSEMBLIES © 2010 A&C Black Publishers Ltd

STORYTELLER
The aliens beeped and wiggled their fingers with delight.
(ACTION AND SOUND.)

ALIENS
You're fantastic! You're amazing!
You are the superstars on Mars!

STORYTELLER
The stars felt so proud of themselves that they twirled and glowed.
(ACTION – STARS TWIRL.)

At last the aliens and robots were ready to leave. They said goodbye to their new friends and prepared to board the spaceship.

(ACTION – EVERYONE SHAKES HANDS AND WAVES.)

Scene 5: We all found there was something we could do

Alina the Alien paused, and said sadly:

ALINA THE ALIEN
I wish we could have helped.

ALIENS
There was *nothing* we could do!

ROBOTS
But you made us proud. (ACTION – PRESS BUTTONS AND WHIRR.)

MOON MONKEYS
You made us happy. (ACTION – BOUNCE.)

STARS
You made us want to shine. (ACTION – TWINKLE.)

ROBOTS, MONKEYS AND STARS
And you had all the good ideas!

STORYTELLER
The aliens felt so proud of themselves that they beeped and wiggled their fingers with joy.
(ACTION – ALIENS BEEP AND WIGGLE FINGERS.)

SONG: WE'RE STUCK ON MARS VARIATION (Original)

EVERYONE:
We fell through the sky,
And crashed with a THUMP!
Our spaceship was broken,
And we got the hump.
How did we help?
We hadn't a clue!
But we all found there was something we could do!

Soon, everyone was back on board Spacebuster 1001.

The captain announced, 'Fasten your seatbelts and prepare for take off!'

10, 9, 8, 7, 6, 5, 4, 3, 2, 1 ... LIFT OFF!

(SOUND EFFECT – ROCKET NOISES.)

The stars twirled and glowed to light the Spacebuster's way and the moon monkeys jumped up and down and waved.

With a mighty ...

WHOOSH!

... the spaceship shot past the stars and disappeared into the blackness of space. Thanks to the superstars on Mars, the aliens were finally on their way home.

Performance Notes

Staging and performance tips (see stage plan)

- **Scene 1:** the Captain sits in his cockpit with Rocky and Robyn on either side of him. The alien passengers sit side by side on a bench behind the Captain, alternately facing left and right. The other two members of the robot crew walk up and down, looking after the passengers on their side of the ship.

- The robots help the alien passengers off the spaceship and into the crater. The aliens gather on the left of the stage, with Arno, Astra, Aggie and Alina at the front. The robots stand to the right of the stage, with Rocky and Robyn at the front. Leave the front of the stage empty for the monkeys. The moon monkeys make a dramatic entrance by either bouncing and chattering down the central audience aisle, or by jumping out from behind the rocks at the front of the stage. They bounce around, then, with the exception of Malvena, sit or crouch down in a line across the front of the stage, backs to the audience.

- **Scene 2:** the robots surround the spaceship as they repair it, cheered on by beeping aliens and bouncing monkeys (seated). When the robots have completed their task, they return to their places on the right.

- **Scene 3:** the monkeys bounce over to the spaceship. They wobble the bench to give the impression that the ship is being moved. Mission completed, the monkeys move back to their places and sit or crouch.

- **Scene 4:** during the song, *Stars shining bright*, the stars stand up on their benches and 'twinkle'.

- **Scene 5:** the crew and passengers say their goodbyes, enter the repaired spaceship and sit in their original places. As the ship takes off, the stars, still standing on their benches, sparkle. The waving monkeys look up as thought they are tracing the passage of the ship into the sky. The aliens and robots look down, wave, and mouth 'goodbye' and 'thank you'.

Scenery

- Make a martian landscape backdrop. Below a dark blue sky, paint or print grey craters. While the paint is still wet, shake patches of red powder paint over the frieze. Add rocks made out of ripped newspaper. Splatter white paint across the sky for stars. Mount on a display board.

- Make two large rocky outcrops by crumpling up several pieces of black sugar paper and sticking them on large pieces of jagged-topped black card. Attach each cluster of rocks to two rounders hurdles.

- Use a PE bench for the spaceship.
  Stick silver or white card along the sides of the bench, with SPACEBUSTER 1001 printed on the side that can be seen. Place the spaceship to the right of the stage pointing towards the centre.

☀ Props

- Use toy tools to mend the spaceship.

- Cover empty drink cans with shiny 'moon juice' labels.

☀ Costumes

- **Robots:** use silver catering plates or trays for the robots' chests. Add buttons, levers and wires. Tie firmly in place with tapes or elastic. Underneath, the robots wear plain black, long-sleeved tops and black trousers. The Captain can wear a gold chest-plate and peaked cap.

- **Aliens:** dress the aliens in plain green, long-sleeved tops and tights and yellow rubber gloves. Help the children to make green headdresses with dangling antennae. Make scaly chest-plates by sticking egg box bases over pieces of card and painting green. Fix in place with tapes or elastic.

- **Moon monkeys:** use plain, brown or yellow long-sleeved tops and matching trousers or tights. Attach ovals of fur fabric to the front of the tops. Make monkey headbands and long tails (plaited tights with frayed ends).

- **Stars:** plain white, long-sleeved tops and tights form the basis of the stars' costumes. Pin or stitch silver or black stars on the front of their tops. Make starry headbands. The stars can wave bunches of tinsel or shine torches as they dance.

☀ Sound effects

- Accompany *Grab a tool* with tapping and sawing sounds.

- A recording of a spaceship taking off would be effective at the end of the play. Alternatively, experiment with the children to find appropriate vocal sounds.

Curriculum Links

Literacy Link
Stories about fantasy worlds.

PSHE

- Talk about the recovery mission of Spacebuster 1001. What skills did each of the four groups of characters provide? Which of these was the most important? Talk about the aliens' contribution to the mission (ideas, encouragement, praise). Why did they think they hadn't done anything to help?

ACTIVITY BOX: CIRCLE TIME

I'm good at: invite the children to say one thing they are good at, and to provide an example of their skill, eg, 'I'm good at making people better, because I read a story to nanny when she was ill'.

S/he's good at: ask the children to talk to the person next to them about his or her talents, then, when invited to speak, each child tells the class what the other person is good at.

Dance and Music

- Move like the characters in *Superstars on Mars*: shuffle and wiggle fingers like the aliens, move jerkily like the robots, bounce like the moon monkeys and twirl and glide like the stars. Rehearse vocal sound effects for each group: alien beeps, robotic chants ('I-am-a-robot'), monkey jumps ('Boing! Boing!') and high-pitched stellar singing (*Twinkle, twinkle little star*).

- Divide the class into two groups (dancers and soundmakers), then further divide the children so that there are are about four aliens, monkeys, robots and stars within each of the two groups. Tell the dancers that they can move only when they hear their sound. Orchestrate the dance by pointing at each group of soundmakers in turn. When the children have got the hang of it, try two sounds/dancing groups together, then three, then all of them. Swap over. Remind the children to sustain high-quality sound and movement.

Science and Geography

- Where is Mars in our galaxy? Ask the children to find out more about Mars.

Design Technology

- Design moon juice labels for the aliens' cans of drink.

Stage Plans

MAGIC in the Classroom

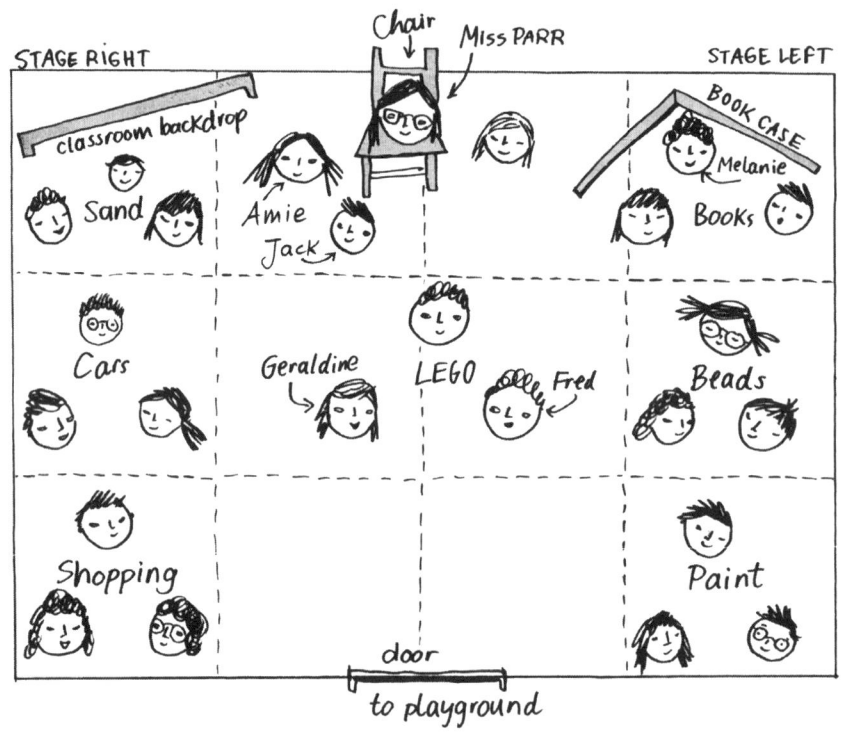

The AWONGALEMA Tree

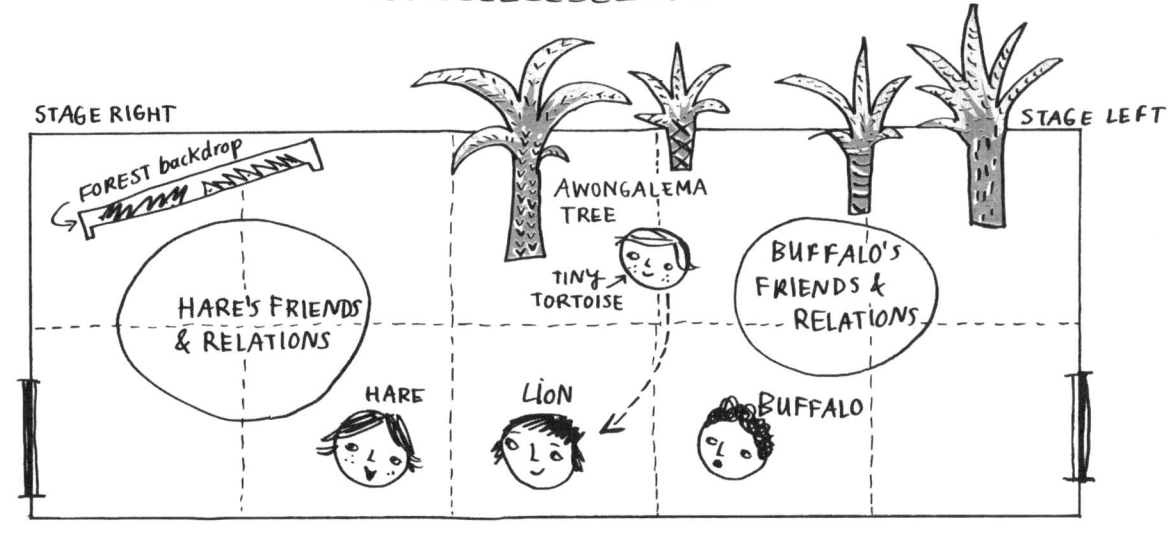

The Enormous Turnip

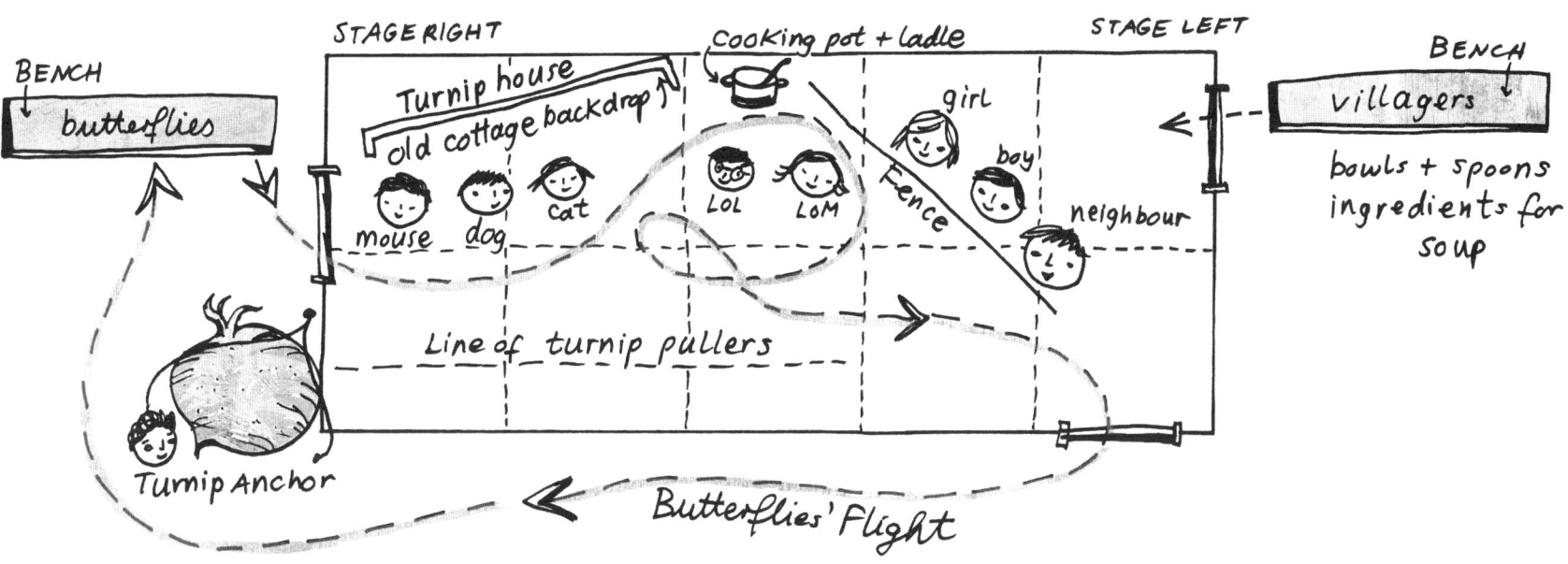

STAGE RIGHT

STAGE LEFT

BENCH
butterflies

BENCH
villagers

bowls + spoons ingredients for soup

Turnip house
old cottage backdrop

Cooking pot + ladle

mouse   dog   cat   LoL   LoM   girl   boy   neighbour

Fence

Line of turnip pullers

Turnip Anchor

Butterflies' Flight

Superstars On Mars

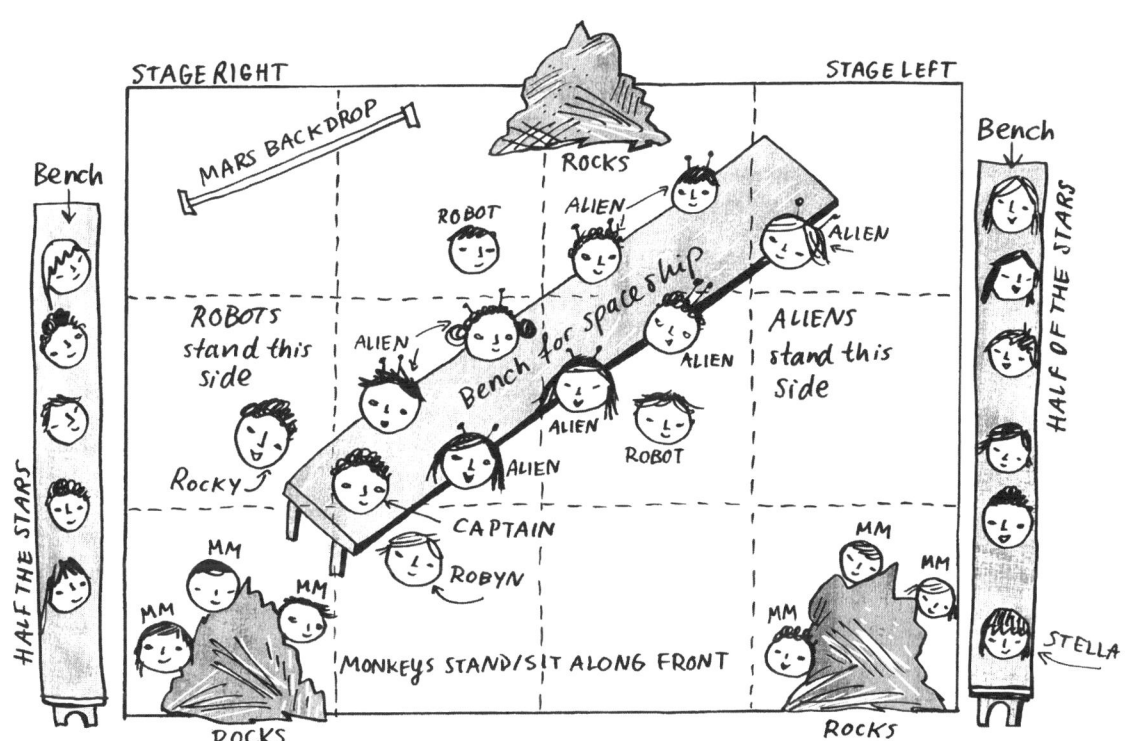

STAGE RIGHT

STAGE LEFT

Bench

Bench

MARS BACKDROP

ROCKS

ROBOT   ALIEN   ALIEN

ALIEN

HALF OF THE STARS

HALF OF THE STARS

ROBOTS stand this side

ALIEN

Bench for spaceship

ALIEN

ALIENS stand this side

Rocky

ALIEN

ROBOT

MM

MM

CAPTAIN

ROBYN

MM

MM

MM

STELLA

ROCKS

MONKEYS STAND/SIT ALONG FRONT

ROCKS

SEAL Links

☼ Magic in the Classroom

New beginnings
I know that I belong to a community.
The story is about a class community.
I know what I have to do myself to make the classroom and school a safe and fair place for everyone, and that it is not OK for other people to make it unsafe or unfair.
The children are urged to listen to the teacher and to do as they are asked. The children suffer the consequences of four children who don't conform to this rule.
I can help to make the class a safe and fair place.
In the second part of the story, the class becomes a happier place when all the children listen and do as they are asked.
I can help to make my class a good place to learn.
The class becomes a better place to learn when everyone is listening.

Getting on and falling out (Y1/2)
I can listen well to other people when they are talking.
In the second part of the play, the four children demonstrate that they are capable of listening and doing as they are asked straight away.

☼ The Awongalema Tree

Going for goals
I can say what I want to happen when there is a problem (set a goal).
Lion knows what has to be done when the animals are starving, and explains it to the animals.
I can predict and understand the consequences of my solutions or ideas.
Lion knows that all will be well if the animals can learn the magic word to make the Awongalema tree bear fruit.
I can choose a realistic goal.
Lion's goal is realistic – but he doesn't take account of the character weaknesses of Hare, Buffalo and himself.
I can resist distractions.
Tiny Tortoise is the only animals who managed to resist distractions.

The Enormous Turnip

Getting on and falling out (Y1/2)

I can work well in a group.

The villagers and animals work well as a team to pull up the turnip. The little old lady and the little old man work well together – one cooks, the other carves a home.

Going for goals

I can say what I want to happen when there is a problem (set a goal).

The little old lady knows exactly what she and her husband want – food and a home.

I can think of lots of different ideas or solutions.

The little old lady has several good ideas and solutions – dig up the turnip, enlist the help of neighbours and animals, make soup, carve out a house and reward the helpers.

I can predict and understand the consequences of my solutions or ideas.

The little old lady has a good idea of the benefits of digging up the turnip.

I can choose a realistic goal.

The little old lady sets a tough goal, but is optimistic of achieving it – with a little help from her friends.

Superstars on Mars

Getting on and falling out (Y1/2)

I can make someone feel good by giving them a compliment.

The aliens are very good at praising the skills of the robots, moon monkeys and stars, and it is clear that their compliments are appreciated.

Going for goals

I can say what I want to happen when there is a problem (set a goal).

The aliens are good at explaining what has to be done to get the spaceship back into space.

I can think of lots of different ideas or solutions.

The aliens are full of ideas.

I can predict and understand the consequences of my solutions or ideas.

The aliens are right every time when it comes to predicting the consequences of their ideas.

Good to be me

I can tell you ... something that makes me feel proud/about my gifts and talents.

Thanks to the compliments paid by the aliens, the robots, monkeys and stars are all aware of their talents and proud of them.

I can tell you when I feel proud.

The aliens feel proud when their talents are pointed out to them.

I can help another person feel proud/I can use the problem-solving process.

The aliens are good at both of these things.

Melody Lines

Magic in the Classroom

A busy classroom

We're play - ing in the sand,_____ We're play - ing in the sand._____
We're look - ing at some books,_____ We're look - ing at some books._____

We're hav - ing fun to - day, We're play - ing in the sand._____
We're hav - ing fun to - day, We're look - ing at some books._____

What a pity

What a pi - ty, what a pi - ty, It's no fun at school to - day. One or

two won't stop to lis - ten to what the teach - er has to say.

Happy days

If we all do as we're asked, And do it straight a-way, We

don't waste time,___ We learn a lot,___ And have a hap-py day. We

don't waste time,___ We learn a lot,___ And have a hap-py day.

The Awongalema Tree

Hungry

Hun - gry, so hun - gry, Our tum - mies are emp - ty. Long weeks of sun - shine With no sign of rain.

Hun - gry, so hun - gry, Our tum - mies are emp - ty. Send us some food to fill them a - gain.

Mighty Mountain Spirit

There's a Migh - ty Moun - tain Spi - rit in a cave, There's a

Migh - ty Moun - tain Spi - rit in a cave. Go and tell it we're in trou - ble, Then

come back at the dou - ble, And we'll clap you on the back for be - ing brave!

Melody Lines – THE AWONGALEMA TREE

The Enormous Turnip

I'm a great big turnip

| D | | G | D | Em | D | A⁷ | D |

(1) I'm a great big tur - nip, Fat and round. See me grow - ing In the ground.
(2) I'm a great big tur - nip, Fat and round. See me grow - ing In the ground.

| D | | G | D | Bm | G | A⁷ | D |

When I've fin - ished grow - ing, Give a shout! Make some soup And pour it out.
When I've fin - ished grow - ing, Give a shout! Cut a door And scoop me out.

Little house

We're glad, ve-ry glad, That we have a lit-tle house, We've got room for our friends, And the dog and cat and mouse. And it's fit for a king, And it's fit___ for a queen, It's the nic-est lit-tle tur-nip house We've ev-er seen.

Superstars on Mars

We're stuck on Mars

We fell through the sky,___ And crashed with a THUMP! Our space-ship is bro-ken, And we've got the hump. Please can you help___ us? We have-n't a clue!___ We're stuck on Mars and there's no-thing we can do!

Melody Lines – THE ENORMOUS TURNIP/SUPERSTARS   CLASS ASSEMBLIES © 2010 A&C Black Publishers Ltd

If you're handy and you know it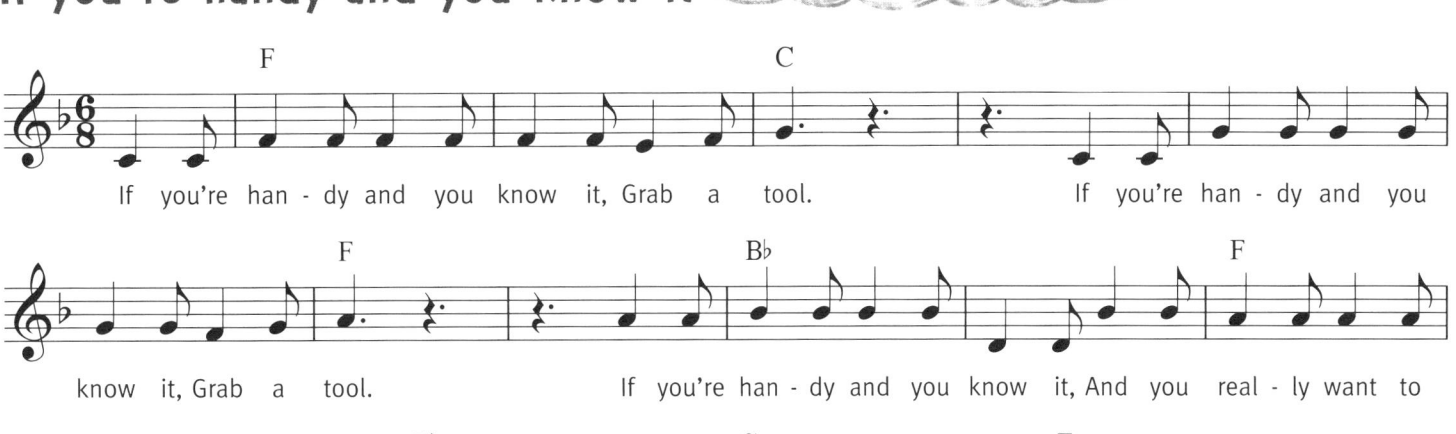

If you're han-dy and you know it, Grab a tool. If you're han-dy and you

know it, Grab a tool. If you're han-dy and you know it, And you real-ly want to

show it, If you're han-dy and you know it, Grab a tool.

Jump, jump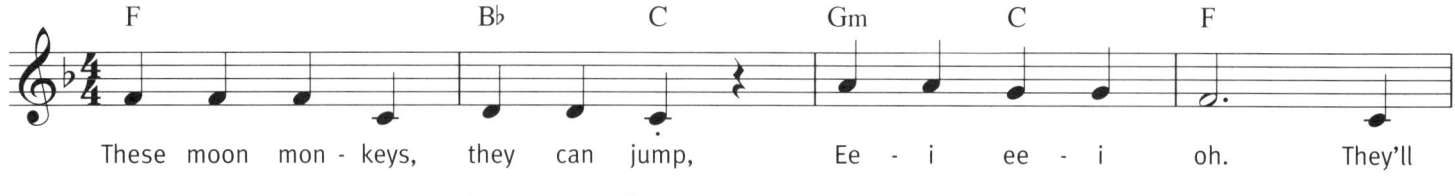

F   Bb   C   Gm   C   F

These moon mon - keys, they can jump, Ee - i ee - i oh. They'll

Bb   C   Gm   C   F

move this space - ship with a thump, Ee - i ee - i oh. With a

great jump here, And a great jump there. Here a jump, There a jump, Ev -'ry - where a jump, jump.

Bb   C   Gm   C   F

These moon mon - keys, they can jump, Ee - i - ee - i oh.

Melody Lines – *SUPERSTARS ON MARS*

Stars shining bright

Stars shin-ing bright in the dark-ness of space. Shine, shine and glow we go,

Shine, shine and glow we go, Shine, shine and glow we go, Twink-ling with grace.

We're stuck on Mars (variation)

We fell through the sky,___ And crashed with a THUMP!_ Our

space-ship was bro-ken, And we got the hump. How did we help?_ We

had-n't a clue!_ But we all found there was some-thing we could do!

And finally ...

Performance licence information

To present an informal performance of any of the class assemblies from this publication, you do not need to purchase a separate performance licence. An informal performance is a performance, with or without an audience, that takes place within an educational establishment or church, where box office takings are less than £250.

You may also make copies of the audio CD solely for the purpose of preparing for and aiding an informal performance within the establishment for which the original script was purchased without paying a further fee. Any copies made must not be distributed outside of the establishment for which the original script was purchased, and must be destroyed once the performance has taken place. Any other copying is strictly prohibited.

If you wish to video or record a performance, either for your own internal use or in order to sell copies to parents, you must write to us separately to obtain permission. See below for our contact details.

If you wish to present a performance of any of the class assemblies from this publication where any box office takings will exceed £250, you must contact us for permission and an appropriate performance licence:
The Copyright Manager
Music Department
A&C Black Publishers Ltd
36 Soho Square
London W1D 3QY
music@acblack.com

About the authors

Veronica Clark is author of *High Low Dolly Pepper* (A&C Black), *The Raggedy King* (Starshine Music), and co-author of *Three Little Nativities* and *Three Little Celebrations* (A&C Black). She was music advisor to the BBC WATCH programme, *The Song Catcher*, and is a former primary headteacher and specialist in music education for pre-school and infant children. She believes that involving children in musicals provides them with an exciting and relevant educational experience, which encourages them to experience all areas of the curriculum.

Kaye Umansky taught for fourteen years in London primary schools, specialising in drama and music. She has been a full-time children's author for the last twenty-five years and has written many plays, music books and novels, including the *Pongwiffy* series (Bloomsbury), *Three Tapping Teddies*, *Three Singing Pigs*, *Three Rocking Crocs*, and the award-winning *Three Rapping Rats* (A&C Black), and is also co-author of *Three Little Nativities* and *Three Little Celebrations* (A&C Black). She lives in London with her husband, daughter and two cats.

Pippa Goodhart went from bookselling into writing, and has had over seventy children's books published since then, ranging from picture books, through early readers to novels. Her picture book *You Choose* has sold three quarters of a million copies, and is one of Bookstart's chosen books for three year-olds. Her novels have been shortlisted for six major awards. She also writes as Laura Owen when writing the *Winnie the Witch* stories. She combines writing with teaching both children and adults.

Jenny McLachlan is an Advanced Skills English teacher who works in East Sussex. She has written stories for children and teenagers and has created a wide range of English teaching resources. Through her work, she is involved in educational research and promoting good teaching practice in primary and secondary schools. She has a passion for children's literature and a belief that it is through engaging with imaginative writing that children learn about their world.

Acknowledgements

Story of *Magic in the Classroom* © 2010 Veronica Clark
Songs: *A busy classroom* and *What a pity*, words © Veronica Clark, music traditional
Happy days, words and music © Veronica Clark
Story of *The Awongalema Tree* © 2010 Kaye Umansky
Songs: *Mighty Mountain Spirit*, words © Kaye Umansky, music traditional
Hungry, words and music © Kaye Umansky
Go like the wind, words © Kaye Umansky
Story of *The Enormous Turnip* © 2010 Pippa Goodhart
Songs: *I'm a great big turnip*, words © Pippa Goodhart, music traditional
Little house, words © Pippa Goodhart and Veronica Clark, music traditional
Heave Ho! words © Veronica Clark
Story of *Superstars on Mars* © 2010 Jenny McLachlan
Songs: *If you're handy and you know it*, *Jump, jump* and *Stars shining bright*, words © Jenny McLachlan, music traditional
We're stuck on Mars, words and music © Jenny McLachlan

Teaching activities © 2010 Veronica Clark

Cover illustration © 2010 Tim Hopgood
Cover design by Jane Tetzlaff and Sara Oiestad
Inside illustrations © 2010 Christiane Engel
Edited by Lucy Mitchell
Text design by Fiona Grant
Music setting by Jeanne Roberts
Recorded arrangements, incidental music, sound engineering and mastering by Matthew Moore
Songs sung by Kaz Simmons

The publishers and authors would like to thank the following people:
Pashley Down Infant School
Year 1: Kim Cherry and pupils in Otters, Nicola Perrin and pupils in Foxes, Liz Williams and pupils in Moles, Louise Alleyne and pupils in Badgers.
Shinewater County Primary
Moira Smith-Nicholls.

First published 2010
A&C Black
36 Soho Square, London W1D 3QY
© 2010 A&C Black
ISBN: 978-1-4081-2456-7
Printed in Great Britain by Caligraving Ltd, Thetford, Norfolk